To: Tucker, Sadie & Rosy,

You make Seaside magical! ♡

Seaside
A to Z

by Katie Hines Porterfield

Katie H. Porterfield

Art by Liza Snyder

Liza Snyder

ACKNOWLEDGMENTS

We would like to thank Daryl Davis, co-founder of Seaside, who gave us permission to use this special town as our subject and inspiration. A huge thank you also goes out to the Seaside businesses that allowed us to use their names and likenesses.

Seaside A to Z

©2020 Katie Hines Porterfield.

Art by Liza Snyder
Book Design by Circa Design

For more information, please contact:
Mascot Books
620 Herndon Parkway, Suite 320
Herndon, VA 20170
info@mascotbooks.com

Library of Congress Control Number: 2020909283

CPSIA Code: PRT0720A
ISBN: 978-1-64543-580-8

Printed in the United States

To Jim, Sue, and their grandchildren.

Katie

To all the artists, young and old, on 30A. You inspire me!

Liza

In the Florida panhandle on scenic Highway 30A,
there's an extra special town where families love to play.

Seaside, they call it; it's a paradise through and through,
with its sugar-white sand and its water turquoise-blue.

It's known for pastel houses, which you'll notice off the bat,
and a beloved restaurant named for a dog and a cat.

There's a cute little post office and a chapel oh-so-sweet,
and more great spots to dine as you wander down the street.

When folks come to visit, they really like to shop,
and the open-air market is a popular stop.

Picket fences, sandy footpaths, house names, and more;
there's so much that's unique about this place I adore.

So, join me as I show you just how fun Seaside can be;
let's take a mini tour and explore from A to Z.

Look for
me on
every page!

Airstreams line the street for a quick bite to eat.

Riding Bikes all over town can't be beat.

Egrets and gulls
like me might try
to steal your snack.

But we really like Fish, so you best watch your back.

Kids run wild on the amphitheater Green.

Which of these **Houses** was on the "big screen"?

Shave **I**ce is refreshing in the summer sun.

The Gulf breeze helps Kites get off the ground.

Lucky Locals get to live here year-round!

Modica Market has lots of yummy finds.

Naps near the water rest our bodies and minds.

And fun at the Pool is always in reach.

Head to Sundog Books to find a good beach read.

Duckies has a Toy that suits every kid's need.

Underwater there are creatures galore.

Yogurt, fudge, or ice cream? You get to decide.

AUTHOR

Katie Hines Porterfield

A writer based in Nashville, Katie Hines Porterfield created A to Z Children's Books to capture what people love about places that make them happy. She relies on talented artists with a connection to each locale to bring her words to life, giving each book a style that's as unique as the place itself. Her growing brand of books includes *Sewanee A to Z, Find Your Heart in Lake Martin: An A to Z Book, The Homestead A to Z, Smith Lake A to Z, Cape Charles A to Z,* and *The Sewanee Night Before Christmas.* Katie, her husband Forrest, and their twin boys, Hines and Shep, enjoy spending time with family and friends in Seaside (and all over 30A), so publishing this book was a longtime goal. She holds a B.A. in American Studies from Sewanee: The University of The South and an M.A. in journalism from the University of Alabama. Purchase her books at atozchildrensbooks.com and follow her on Instagram and Facebook @atozchildrensbooks

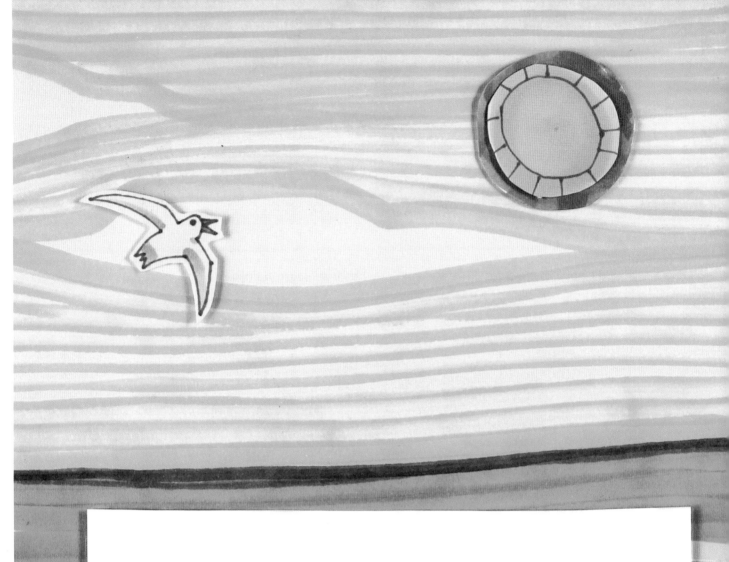

ARTIST

Liza Snyder

Liza Snyder lives just north of Seaside in the historic neighborhood of Point Washington. She is a practicing artist and teaches art workshops for kids and grown-ups in her studio. Liza delights in exploring different art mediums, and this book is her first time working as an illustrator. A native of both Mobile, Alabama, and St. Simons Island, Georgia, her childhood near the water prepared her for a quiet life near 30A. Liza shares her light and life with Jeremy, Maysie, Cobb, and Ruthie, who are all artists as well! Check out her work on lizasnyder.com and follow her on Instagram and Facebook @lizasnyderart